Survival

SYLVIA McNICOLL

HIP Mainstreet
Copyright © 2014 by Sylvia McNicoll

LIBRARY AND ARCHIVES CANADA CATALOGUING IN PUBLICATION

McNicoll, Sylvia, 1954-, author
    Survival / Sylvia McNicoll.

(HIP mainstreet)
ISBN 978-1-926847-54-2 (pbk.)

    I. Title.

PS8575.N52S87 2014   jC813'.54   C2014-902465-7

General editor: Paul Kropp
Text design: Laura Brady
Illustrations drawn by: Greg Ruhl
Cover design: Robert Corrigan

1 2 3 4 5 6 7   19 18 17 16 15 14

Printed and bound in Canada

High Interest Publishing acknowledges the financial support of the Government of Canada through the Canada Book Fund for our publishing activities.

When a small plane crashes in the bush, teenage Sky and her younger brother are mostly unhurt. But their mother is badly injured and Doc only has the use of one arm. When no help arrives, Sky has to overcome fear, cold and despair to save her mother's life.

Chapter 1
Be Careful What You Wish For

"FIFTY PERCENT OF all marriages end in divorce,"
Doc Joe says. He's lifting his medical bag into the
back of the plane. "It seems awful now. But lots of
kids go through it. You can survive this too."

"Sure." I sniff.

I'm not crying, it's just cold outside. Minus 19.
The horizon glows a fiery orange. In five hours the
same bright line will turn into sunset.

Too short a day, too long a night, says my father.
It's part of our family problem.

Dad is already waiting for us down south. We
fly from there to Vancouver, then onto Los Angeles.

"Sky?" Doc Joe turns towards me.

It's my name. The name was my father's cute idea. My brother's is Land. If they had another kid, he was going to name it Lake. Sometimes I call my dad Mud, just to get even.

Doc's mouth is smiling, but his brown eyes are sad.

I shrug at him and hoist up a box. The box has my room stuff: a teddy bear made out of muskox fur, a dream catcher, and a book called *Zombie Polar Bear*. Junk reading. Of course there's my laptop and a framed photo of my best friend, Josée.

Not a lot to show for my seventeen years. Still, I try on a smile for Doc.

He's cool. Doc is Mom's childhood friend from the Reserve. I want to believe him about surviving this divorce. But my brother Land and I are not like "lots of kids." Not our names, not our situation. "We have to leave everything we've ever known." I throw one of my mother's bags in the back, hard, like that will make anything better. "Do other kids have to do that?"

"Some. But you'll be back for visits."

"I don't want to leave. Why can't she let me stay with her?"

"It's such a big world out there. Your mother wants you to see it all. Then you can choose to live here." Doc Joe lifts another case into the plane. Dad's told me all this before. I didn't believe him either.

"She just doesn't want to be bothered looking after me." I lift Land's box of toys in. Why isn't he out here helping?

"A bush pilot like your mom never gets regular hours." Doc shrugs. "And teenagers can get into so much trouble when there's nothing to do and no one around to supervise."

Okay, I can see why they would think that. Last month Josée got pregnant. But I don't even have a boyfriend, so no worries for Mom there. And sure Mike and Hank, two losers in the grade behind me, got caught sniffing gas, which I don't get at all. With all the Ski-Doos flying around at night, why do they have to sniff it? They can just breathe in the night air.

She should know that I'm not like them. I have plans, but they don't include living in Vancouver.

"I can fly with Mom. Train to be a pilot. Her co-pilot. Look at me, loading the plane. I'm her personal rampie half the time anyways."

"So am I. Come on, Sky," he says gently. "You have school. You're better off with your dad. This is so much worse for your mom."

"Yeah, well she could stop it—I can't. I hate her. I wish she would die."

Dr. Joe holds up one mitted hand in a silent stop sign. I have gone too far even for him. He frowns, eyes looking beyond my shoulder. I know it before I turn around. Mom stands there with Land's hand in hers.

They both have heard me.

My brother wears a silly sock monkey hat. It makes him look even younger than seven, and he's a pale little kid anyway. His mouth hangs open.

He's got a tooth missing at the bottom, and a loose one next to it he likes to wiggle for effect. His big eyes ask questions but I can't answer. He doesn't know the truth yet. All Mom told him about was Disneyland, which is where we're spending the holidays. It will be our last Christmas together as a family. Mickey Mouse, Donald Duck, Pirates of the Caribbean. And Land doesn't know . . . yet.

Sorry, I say in my head but I can't force the words out of my mouth. *I didn't mean it.* I don't hate Mom. What I hate is having no say over the most important things in my life.

Too many moments pass, and Mom pretends she never heard. "Land, you sit behind me," she tells my brother.

"Aw, why can't I sit in the front with you?" With his hands he pretends to guide a steering wheel. "Be the co-pilot."

"Because little kids aren't safe in the front," I tell him. I grab his shoulders and push him to the back.

He shrugs me off.

"Sky, you sit behind Doc," Mom says. "That will balance the weight."

I stare into her eyes for an extra few seconds. Dark, like mine. *Why can't I sit in the front with you?* It could be the last time in a long while. But if I say anything, I will sound like my little brother and I'm seventeen. Mom's eyes look soft, teary. She glances down and then continues her walk around the plane.

"It's always safest in the back," Doc says as he gets into the co-pilot seat. "Nothing to do with being little."

Mom shuffles some of our packing and then climbs up into the cockpit. Doc and Mom put the headsets on and the engine turns over, the prop spins. Once Mom gets the clearance for takeoff, the plane moves forward, faster and faster.

Just like our life.

And then it lifts off. I love this moment. Everything below becomes small and far away. It's as though we could reach down, pick up the trucks parked in the lot below and put them in a Christmas stocking. The long buildings and houses become toys in patchwork quilts and then they disappear behind us. Scruffy fir trees cling to the rocks in between the stretches of pure white. The snow looks silent and clean. The sunlight bounces off it in diamonds.

Mom nudges Doc Joe on the shoulder and points out the window. He nods and smiles. "Look over there!"

"Santa's reindeer!" Land squeals. Living in the North, most kids give up early on Santa. They know there's no building full of elves at the North Pole. But Land will believe in anything that gets him more stuff.

Santa's reindeer are really caribou running across a frozen lake. The shadow of our airplane divides the herd. They scatter around the shadow. I can't help smiling too, taking a picture of it in my head. Who knows when I'll see caribou running free like that again?

At the edge of the trees I spot him. A lone wolf is watching those caribou too. Will he chase them, all by himself? Does he have friends somewhere on the other side? It's usually the only way wolves can hunt a large animal, using their whole pack. I'll never know what happens to him or those caribou.

Suddenly, Land calls out, "Look at me, look at me!"

He's being a goof. I can tell by the tone of his voice. I should ignore him. I should just keep watching that lone wolf. But I feel sorry for what I said before. I feel bad for what Land will find out in Disneyland. So I turn from the window to my brother's jack-o'-lantern grin. He's lost another tooth!

My stomach does an instant lurch when I see the tiny dugout of blood where his tooth used to be.

"Sky's going to be sick! Sky's going to be sick!" Land sings.

Chapter 2
Crash Position

UP NORTH, IT'S not good to feel queasy about blood. Any food that doesn't get flown in or carted in on a truck, gets hooked, speared or shot. Hunters always cart in their kill strapped to their sleds. They gut their fish in the open, peel the hide off an arctic hare in the yard. Blood is everywhere. You can't hide from it.

Josée wanted me to help skin the muskox she made my teddy bear from. I just couldn't. I ate the muskox pot roast her mom made later, no problem. I just couldn't handle the dead animal.

"Stop it, Land! I'm not going to be sick." Looking at that little bit of blood in Land's mouth made my head swirl, but I don't let on.

Doc Joe passes me a plastic bag. "Just in case." He winks.

I throw it at my brother.

"Ow. Mom! Sky hit me."

Mom keeps her eyes straight ahead.

"She's flying the plane, Land. Shut up."

Land settles back down. He looks out the window quietly for about two seconds till he turns to me again. "Will the Tooth Fairy come to see me in Edmonton tonight?"

"For sure," I answer. The little con artist doesn't believe in the Tooth Fairy, not really. He just likes to pocket the five bucks Mom leaves under the pillow. "She flies just as much as Mom. Lots of stops too."

Before landing in Yellowknife, we're doing a quick pick-up at Diamond Lodge. The ice tourists want to mail some parcels back to Japan and Europe. And Doc's going to check on someone's cough and rib fracture.

"Look, it's snowing!" Land says.

"Pretty, huh?" I say.

Gentle feathers of white drift around the plane. I love that. It's like we're flying in a snow globe that a giant shook very gently.

I see my mother crane her neck to look up through the windshield. She grumbles something about the weather changing.

"Amy, should we bunk down at the lodge?" Doc asks her.

That would be great, I think. The lodge has an outdoor hot tub the size of a small lake. I love being in a pool outside at night with snow falling.

"Nah." Mom shakes her head. "We don't want to miss that flight out of Yellowknife. As long as we can see . . ."

The snow swirls around us now, still gentle. The air becomes fuzzy.

"They don't have snow in California," Land says as he watches the window.

Not much in Vancouver either, I think. "Enjoy it now!" I tell him.

Of course the snow falls harder, swirling so we can only see patches of ground.

The plane bumps a little, no biggie. I don't get airsick. I've been flying since I was a baby.

Doc turns to Mom. He touches her arm.

That touching is just a nice friendship thing, I say to myself. They've known each other since they were kids.

But then I watch his lips move. He lowers his voice so I can't hear him. "I trust you." That's what it looks like he says. What's not to trust? She's the best pilot in the North.

The plane suddenly bucks like we've hit a rock. It's bad.

"I'm going to try to fly around this," Mom calls out loudly so Land and I can hear too.

The plane banks to the left, and the world turns on its side. We continue to bump, only harder now.

Mom's hands tighten on the steering wheel. The snow seems to thicken around us. "I have to fly under this," she says.

She needs to see land to bring us down. It only makes sense. The lodge doesn't have an air traffic controller to guide us in.

Doc Joe nods.

He trusts her. That's what he told her, not two seconds ago. My stomach drops along with the plane. We must be in trouble if he needs to tell her that.

The nose of the Cessna points down. The clouds break away. We can almost touch the tree tops now. Where is Diamond Lodge? Nowhere in sight.

Mom starts to pull up when WHOMP we're hit with wind shear.

The music of the engine suddenly stops. There's an eerie moment of total silence. The moment seems to last forever, but then Mom starts shouting.

"Mayday. Mayday. Mayday!" Mom calls as she steers hard. "This is Raven 521. Our engine has stalled. We are going down!"

"Crash position!" I yell at Land. I push his head to his knees.

Branches scrape wildly across the window. *That's good,* I tell myself. Mom is slowing the plane down. She's using the trees like brakes.

I know she's picked a good soft landing place. It's what she always does. She looks for open spaces just in case. Just in case of . . . this.

I bury my head in my lap and cover it with my hands.

"Mom will save us. Mom will save us. Mom will . . ."

Chapter 3
Getting Out Alive

TICK, TICK, HISS.

In some kind of dream, I open my eyes and see blurry faces. Who are they? And what's that smell? "I don't want to sniff gas," I tell Mike and Hank, the guys from school. I can't make out their faces, but it must be them, the guys always hitting on me. Who else could it be?

But I'm not at school. I'm . . . where? I wrinkle my nose at the thick oily smell.

"It wrecks your brain," I say to no one . . . someone.

Tick, tick, hiss.

Then I hear a voice.

"Sky, help me! I'm scared!"

That's not Mike or Hank's voice. It's someone . . . someone I know.

Geez, it's freezing in here, someone should shut the window. My brain already feels wrecked, like it's been thrown in a blender. A brain smoothie. Ha, ha! I close my eyes again and smile through the pain.

"Sky! Sky!" Someone shakes my shoulder. He's sobbing. I can hear him sucking snot back into his nose.

My eyes open again. A wind blows at me from my right. Why is there no wall there?

Then I see two faces. The two faces look the same . . . wait a minute. They're one face! I realize I'm seeing double. I blink and try to make the two become one. And there's that sound again.

Tick, tick, hiss.

"Mom's hurt really bad. Doc Joe, too." It's my little brother. He's a mess, tears streaming down his face.

"Land?" I should hug him, but it's like I'm floating in a vat of whale oil. My thoughts form slowly.

Tick, tick, hiss.

That's the sound of something wet dripping onto a very hot engine. I see the gaping hole to my right and remember, we crashed! The plane crashed! My heart stops beating for a second, then drums so hard I can hear it outside my body.

The smell is spilled fuel.

We've got to get out of here before we blow up! I think. Only the words don't come out of me. Lifting my head makes the cockpit spin in front of my eyes.

C'mon, Sky, you can do this, I say to myself. Get moving.

I can't pass out. I have to get everyone out of the plane, starting with my brother.

I lower my head between my knees. I take a breath, blink hard. That's better. Only one face stares back into mine.

"Are you okay, Land?"

He's not. He's howling like a wolf cub.

I want to throw back my head and howl too. *What are we going to do?* What am I going to do? There are no adults able to help us. I have to take charge. "I'm sorry, Land, but I need you to be a big boy today. You're going to have to help me. Can you take your seat belt off?"

Land cries more softly, hiccuping as he talks. "It's . . . already . . . off. My . . . arm . . . hurts."

"Can you move it?"

"Yes. Mom won't answer me."

I clench my teeth. I don't want to look her way. The pilot and co-pilot always get the worst in a crash.

"She's probably sleeping," I tell him. "That's the best thing for someone who's hurt. What about Doc?"

"He's making funny noises."

I have to be a big girl today, too, I tell myself. First, I take a breath and make tight fists. My head hurts but nothing swirls. *There's going to be blood.* We need to hurry, but I have to go slow so I don't faint.

The plane is tilted to the pilot side with the nose crushed into the snow. When I stand, I shuffle up against Land, toward Mom.

In front of me, Mom's head is slumped onto the steering yoke. There's blood, but not too much.

I can handle this, I tell myself. *I can stop my hands from shaking and do what I have to do.* My fingers touch the top of Mom's throat. I feel something! That small bumping underneath her jaw, I'm hoping that is her pulse, not mine. I bend over so that I can listen for her breath. That's when I see the blood running down the side of her face. Everything inside me drops, and I start to sink back.

"Wake up, Sky! You can't sleep now." Land pushes at my back to keep me up.

I feel sick but manage to stay awake. "Sorry. I'm okay." *I'm not going to get sick,* I tell myself. But I'm not okay, and neither is Mom.

I look down and see most of Mom's body is pinned under the instrument panel. She's trapped. I slide back up to Doc Joe's side.

He groans and stirs.

"Doc, Doc!" I call to him.

"Get it off!" he groans. His head lifts up but the panel crushes down on him too.

"Can you take your seat belt off?" I ask him.

Doc's eyes blink open. There's a moment when I'm not sure he understands me.

"I want to pull you out, but we need to unsnap your belt."

He moans and seems to struggle. "I . . . I can't. My left hand is broken and . . . and my right arm."

My brother starts to sob again.

I grab Land's arm and hold it tight. "Listen, go look in the back for the survival kit. There's a saw in it." An ax might work better or faster at least but I know Mom doesn't have one. "A saw is way safer," she told me once.

Still, I can use the saw to hack off the two steering yokes. Then it should be easy to pull Mom and Doc Joe free.

Meanwhile I reach around the seat and find the seat buckle. It's stuck of course.

"Got it!" Land's still sniffling but way calmer. "Won't sawing cause a spark?" he asks.

A blade against metal, the kid is right! A spark hitting the fuel could kill us all. "So never mind the saw. Is there a knife?"

"Yup."

"Take it out of the sheath and hand it to me." I reach back with one arm and my hand closes around the handle. I touch Land's fingers and want to squeeze them, to hug my little brother closely. "It's going to be okay," I tell him.

"I can't be a baby," he tells himself.

"That's right." Land has to know how bad this is. He remembered about the spark after all. I reach around Doc's waist and carefully saw at the seat belt with the knife. It's sharp. When the blade bites through the last bit it springs up but touches nothing.

Phew! No spark and I didn't stab Doc, either.

"Can you stand up, Doc? I'm going to pull you out."

He leans hard against the seat and groans. "No. No, I'm stuck."

"What if you move his seat back?" Land asks.

My little brother is a genius! Just like in a car, there's a bar behind Joe's feet that can move the seat backwards. With the panel squeezed in on him, I can't reach that bar. But I can tilt the seat back from the side. At last I reach that lever and push down hard. It's stiff.

The seat releases and it flings back. Doc screams as he falls flat against it.

Not good, I think.

Shifting toward the hole at the side of the plane, I reach to grab him.

Doc groans. "Stop! I have to do it myself." He

slides back slowly. As soon as his knees are free, he rolls out and drops out through the hole.

He lies in the snow motionless. I have to hope he's still alive. We're going to need him to save Mom. To save ourselves.

Chapter 4
Shelter

"IS DOC OKAY?" Land asks.

"Sure," I lie. Doc doesn't look too good, but I don't have time to go out and check. "Why don't you throw down his medical bag? Do you see it back there?"

"I've got it." He walks back to the hole and pitches it out.

"Good boy." My mouth feels paper dry, my tongue swollen like a log. I find it hard to swallow. "Hey, did you see my backpack? I've got a bottle of water in there."

After a minute, Land nudges me with it, and I take out the water. I want to chug the whole thing all at once but only take a couple of swallows, then I pass it to him. When Land downs half the bottle, I grab his arm to stop him. He looks like he's going to cry again.

"Save some for Doc, now. We'll find more later."

Land nods and passes the bottle back so I can cap it.

I've got to get Mom free, but I need something for Land to do. Busy-work will keep Land calm, I hope.

"Why don't you empty the plane? Throw down everything that's useful."

Tick, tick, hiss! The hot engine continues to melt the falling snow. The sound reminds me—any moment the plane may blow. Maybe I should make Land go stand with Doc. But we'll need clothes and food and water and shelter if we want to survive. If all our bags explode with the plane, we die too. Just more slowly.

Most of all I need to get Mom out. She's in no shape to help me. I can't even see her chest rise and fall. She's breathing though, barely. She has to be.

"What's not useful?" Land calls from the back of the Cessna.

"I don't know. Just hurry!"

Carefully, I lower Mom's seat. It jerks back anyway. But she's lying flat now so I can slide her out.

She moans. *Moaning is good, it means she's alive*, I tell myself.

"Sorry, Mom." My hand shakes as I saw at her seat belt. When I cut all the way through, I drop the knife and grab her under the arms.

Mom's a slim lady, maybe 120 pounds, and she's tall. But right now she's dead weight. I might as well be lifting a polar bear. I pull at her with everything I've got but can't budge her.

She moans again.

Are her legs crushed under the instrument panel? No, I can't think about that. One thing at a time. Just get her out of the plane.

Can I get Land to help me? He's probably just as strong as I am.

"Land, get the rope out of the back, quick."

I hear him scrambling and then a bright yellow nylon rope lands on my shoulder. I loop it under Mom's arms. "Here, you grab this side of the rope. If you and I pull at the same time, we should be able to get her out. On the count of three—we don't stop. Ready?"

"Okay."

"One . . . two . . . three!

As we strain, her body moves back . . . but only slightly. No matter how hard we pull, we can't get her out.

"Stop! Her legs are caught!" It's Doc at the open side of the plane.

"What are we going to do?"

Doc crawls back in over the co-pilot seat, holding his arms awkwardly out of the way. Then he leans over Mom and calls softly. "Amy, Amy?"

Mom groans.

"You have to wake up. This can't be the end of everything. The kids need you."

I see Mom's face pull together in pain but her eyes don't open.

"Mom, help us," I tell her. "We have to get you out of here, quick."

Her head moves from side to side. Her eyelids lift. Her eyes widen. She understands.

"Can you just try to push yourself backwards? We'll pull you, too."

She seems to get it. Somehow I know she gets it. This time as Land and I tug, her body comes free.

"Don't stop!" I tell Land. "Let's get her outside."

Bump, bump, Mom's broken body clunks against the other seats. I slip my arms under her, then lift her up and stagger out of the side of the plane. We both tumble onto an icy crust of snow.

The world goes black.

From out of that darkness, someone calls to me and shakes my shoulder. "Don't sleep, Sky. We have to get warm."

But the snow chills my back, my head and my legs and I like it. I can't feel anything else. After

a moment my teeth begin to chatter, and I don't like it so much. Land is right. I struggle awake. "Where's the emergency bag?" I sit up and look around. "Let's get the blanket underneath Mom."

Land scrambles to unzip a large duffle bag. He pulls out what looks like a big sheet of aluminum foil. He puts that on the ground and jams it under Mom. I get up and help him lift her onto it. It's a struggle but Mom's only half awake. Judging by all the blood on her face, that's a good thing.

"We should move farther away from the plane," Doc says. His face looks blue. Besides his arms, what other injuries must he have?

"Okay, okay. Here, have some water first." I pass him the bottle, then look around—nothing but snow and fir trees. "Land, we have to set up camp somewhere out of the wind."

"There's a tent in the bag," he tells me.

"That's good!" Around us are plenty of fir trees. Still the wind gusts and tosses snow into our faces. "How about over there?" One place is just as bad as the next, but I point to a cluster of firs near a large rock. It's a good distance away. That should make us safe in case the Cessna blows. The rock, together with those trees, can give us shelter on one side.

"Let's move everything."

"I can help," Doc says. "I can use this arm, but not the hand," he holds up his left arm. "Land, if you put the strap over my left shoulder, I can carry the supplies over there."

My brother hangs the duffle bag on Doc.

"Okay, you and me," I tell him, "let's grab the blanket, and slide Mom to the spot."

I bend over and have to take a deep breath so I don't do a nose dive into the snow. Grabbing the front corners, I direct Land to the back ones. "Slow and careful, so she doesn't slide off."

I back towards those trees where Doc is slumped. He can't even shrug the strap off his shoulder. Mom groans as we move the blanket.

I'm sweating. It's so cold, I can't be sweating . . . and yet I feel the wetness under my parka.

One foot behind the other, Land and I make our way to the trees. The wind tosses another fistful of snow into our faces. My brother pants as we stop. His blue eyes, exactly like my father's, look so full of hope. I have to look away. I can't look at him. I can't look at Mom.

We're in so much trouble, I can't see how we're going to get out of this alive.

Chapter 5
Staying Warm

WHEN MY BROTHER looks at Mom, his lip trembles.

Her face is swollen on the left side where the blood has crusted. Her eyes are closed. She's barely breathing.

Land whimpers so I put my arm around him. Then I tell him a lie, my very best. "Everything's going to be okay, don't worry. Mom just looks bad right now."

Land seems to believe me. That's good.

"Can you help me get this off?" Doc Joe asks.

My brother eagerly lifts the strap from Doc's shoulder. Then he pulls the bag away.

"Now can you get me my bag?" Doc Joe says.

"We're going to give your mom some medicine. It'll help her feel better."

Land runs back to the pile of bags near the plane.

Doc Joe talks softly to me. "Your mother is in shock. And she likely has internal injuries. We have to put her on an IV to get some fluids in her."

We. It dawns on me what Doc really means. "You mean *I* have to do it."

"Yup." He frowns. "My hands are useless. But at least I have a couple of IV bags with me. Wish I had brought more."

When Land brings the medical bag back, Doc gets him to open it. "Can you take those scissors and cut a hole in her sleeve?" he asks me.

"Wrecking her goose down parka," I mumble. "She's gonna love that." Still, I take off my mitts, grab the scissors and snip into the elbow area of the sleeve. I peel back the nylon fabric. I see her shirt and cut it open.

"Good," Doc says, like I'm one of his staff. "First

we're going to give her something for the pain. Wipe down some skin with that rubbing alcohol. Use one of those swabs. Clean your own hands with it first," he adds. As if I should know.

The cold makes my fingers fumble. The rubbing alcohol stings against one of my cuts. But this isn't about me. Gently I wipe at Mom's arm. I inhale the smell of alcohol. This is not the tough part.

"There's the needle. There's the morphine." Doc points with his chin.

I unwrap the needle and draw the medicine into it. Then I take another deep breath. It catches in my throat.

"Don't worry, you can't possibly hurt her . . ."

Any more than she already is, I finish his sentence in my head. I close my eyes, swallow, and then push the needle into her arm.

"Good! Land, how would you like to be the nurse here?" He doesn't wait for my brother to answer. "Grab those two bags, the one with the pouch of liquid, that's it. And the one with the tubing."

"I don't want to be a nurse," Land tells him. "I want to be a fireman."

"Okay. You're a firefighter then. Open that bag with the pouch of liquid. That's your water supply."

Land grins and gets the pouch out.

"Now you need to connect it to the pump and hose. Those are in the other bag." Doc gets Land to connect the IV pouch to the tubing. "See at the top there. That's your pump. You need to switch it on and squeeze it a couple of times to prime it. But first shut the nozzle at the other end so the water doesn't drip out."

Land does as Doc asks him.

"Okay, we're going to let some water run through to the nozzle. Got to make sure there are no air bubbles." We all watch as the liquid runs through the thin clear tubing. "Perfect," Doc says. "You can open the nozzle again, Land. And hold the water supply in the air."

Land hoists up the IV bag.

"Your turn, Sky."

I take a breath. Just what I was afraid of.

"See that blue band in my bag? Tie that above your mom's elbow."

I do as he says, but the band squeezes her arm. "It looks too tight!"

"Has to be. Now you can see the vein just below her elbow. Tap around it. That's it. Wipe that with more rubbing alcohol."

I rub another swab across her forearm.

"Great."

The easy part's done. There's been no real blood . . . not yet.

"Pull the skin tight and angle the needle into her arm. Nice and slow."

I close my eyes. Then I swallow the sick in my throat and take another breath. I can't do it. I can't push the needle in.

"Come on, Sky," Doc says gently. "You have to do this."

I let my breath out and slowly slide the needle in.

As the needle pierces my mom's skin, blood splashes up in the clear tube.

"You've got it! Pull the needle out, push the hub in! Super. Land, pass her some of those packages. You just have to tape the tube in place, Sky."

One by one I open the packages, peel back some sticky squares and cover the IV tube. When I'm done, I connect the tube and take the needle out completely.

"You can untie her arm, too," Doc says.

I remove the blue band. Only then do I wipe the tears from my face.

Doc shows me how to adjust the flow. "Now, can you hang the bag from that branch, Land?"

Land fidgets a bit to get the bag to hold on the twig. When he's done he throws his arms around me and squeezes hard.

"That should last her for a few hours. Rescue crew should find us way before then."

I look up at the sky. There's nothing but swirling whiteness. Can a plane fly in this? Can a pilot see us in this? I look back down at Doc.

His eyes squeeze together. It seems like he's going to pass out. "Sky, can you do me a favor?"

"Sure," I answer. Nothing could be harder than what I just did to my mother.

"Can you give me a shot of that morphine too?"

I groan.

"Please," Doc begs. "I wouldn't ask, but . . ."

I sigh. *Not again.* But I know I have no choice.

This time is only slightly easier. I help Doc pull the parka sleeve down off his shoulder so I only have to cut open his shirt. Dab, wipe, another deep breath and I stab.

As I finish, I have to wonder again, how bad is Doc? Doesn't he need that other IV bag?

"I'm cold," my brother suddenly says.

"Right! Okay. Let's set up that tent you saw."

Land reaches into the bag and pulls out an orange rectangle. It doesn't look big enough for everyone. It doesn't look very strong either.

I tear open the package and check out the

instruction sheet. "Easy peasy to put up," it says. Yeah, sure. I frown as I unfold the tent. It's like a large orange garbage bag with a rope from either end. "You tie this on a branch I guess." I pull one end of the rope to a fir tree next to us, away from Mom's IV bag. Then I loop one end over the highest branch I can reach. The other I hook to the opposite tree. The garbage bag turns into a bright triangle with an entry hole on either end. It's very lightweight.

The wind suddenly hurls the tent up in the air. It's like a sheet on a clothesline.

"What good is that?" I ask.

"Great to keep the sun off. You can use it if you crash in L.A." Doc Joe starts coughing as he laughs. For a while, he can't stop coughing. He turns away.

Land's mouth hangs down as he looks at the flapping orange tent. We both stare at it for a few seconds. It beats looking down at our mom. It beats thinking about where we are.

Doc turns back. "Well, it's bright. Makes us more visible to rescue planes."

I look back at our bags, still lying near the Cessna. "Should we burn all the clothes?"

"No," Doc Joe says. "You may want to change into them or pile them on to stay warm. Break off the lower branches of these trees behind us. They should be dry enough to burn."

Yeah, that's what I saw once on a video. Still, it's something to try. And moving helps us stay warm. When we have a pile of branches up to my waist, I strike a match to the brownest needles at the bottom. Nothing. And again. Nothing.

"We need a starter. Paper would help," Doc Joe says.

"I know just the thing." *Zombie Polar Bear.*

Chapter 6
Saving the Zombies

"WHERE, WHERE?" Land asks. "Where's the zombie bear?"

"No, you goober. It's a book I have in my case. Let's get it."

Zombie Polar Bear is not my usual kind of book. But the author visited our school, and I wanted to get a copy autographed. Only I forgot my money that day. No one loaned me any. Then the class surprised me by buying a copy for my going-away present.

Together, we head back to the plane to get my special book. The nose and pilot side are jammed into the snow, crushed. The wing on the passenger side lies slightly behind it, shorn off by a tree. We survived that. So we should be able to get through the next few hours until a search and rescue team spots us.

The plane is quiet now. There's no hissing sound coming from the engine or any other part of the Cessna.

It can't blow up, anymore, can it? The fuel tanks are stored under both wings. I check the broken one. A large puddle of light blue liquid surrounds the wing right to the fuselage. The avgas. With a cold engine and no other sparks, it shouldn't blow up. We should be safe.

It takes three trips to schlep everything back to the rock. From the bottom of my box, I take out the book *Zombie Polar Bear*. The cover is white, the bear is white. But the title is in shiny red letters to match the shiny blood around his neck. My class gave me it on my last day. I open it to the front page.

For Sky, so you'll always remember us and the North.

The author plus all my friends have signed the book, and I haven't even read it yet. I hate to give it up. I chew my lip. But to stay alive we need those branches to catch.

"Good book?" Doc asks.

I shrug. "Doesn't matter. We can use it to light the fire."

"You don't have to do that," Doc says. "There's a case of toilet paper we were bringing Diamond Lodge. Did you unload that?"

"Really?" I smile with relief. "Didn't see it. Land?"

"I thought it didn't belong to us."

"Well, the Lodge people can wait for their toilet paper," Doc says. "And maybe there are a couple more things."

"Sure," I say, sounding hopeful. I mess up Land's hair with my hand. "Let's go back and see what else is in the plane."

Land squirms, then runs ahead of me back to the Cessna. There's the carton of toilet paper, and one more of cleaning stuff. There are some fancy soaps, bottles of shampoo, and tablets for the Diamond Lodge hot tub.

"No food. Too bad," I say.

"Some hot chocolate in here!" Land holds up a bag.

I look around the back and grab a blue tarp. "This looks like a better emergency tent than that orange thing."

"Here's a shovel," Land calls.

We take our treasures back to the clump of fir trees. With the shovel, we dig a shallow hole for a fire pit. I stand some of the branches upright in the snow around it. Then I thread the tops through the holes at the edge of the tarp. Perfect. We have a windbreak.

"Let's pile the snow up on the side of the tarp," I tell Land. "You shovel. I'll start the fire."

With the toilet paper, the flame should light easily. I strike a match, and the paper blazes for a moment. I hold my breath. Maybe ten needles on a branch glow for about twenty seconds. "Come on, come on!" I beg.

But they go out.

We're turning into something from *Call of the Wildman*. It would be funny if Doc Joe's teeth weren't chattering.

Suddenly a sound in the distance makes all of us look up. It's a large passenger plane—but that doesn't matter. One of the pilots should pick up our transmitter signal. They'll know we're in trouble. Unless . . .

Doc Joe asks the million-dollar question. "Did . . . you check . . . if the ELT . . . was on?" Teeth still chattering.

The ELT is the emergency location transmitter. Once a pilot picks up that signal, he can radio Search and Rescue where we are.

"Wouldn't it go on automatically?" I ask.

"Maybe . . . or your mom could have started it." He paused for a second, thinking. "But it could need . . . a manual reset."

"*Sh--,*" I think, but don't say it. Then I think a few more choice words.

"There's a flare gun in the survival kit!" Land says.

He quickly digs through the kit and whips out a red plastic pistol. Land has been out on a few muskox hunts so he knows how to handle a gun. Before we can say anything, he cracks it in half, loads it, and aims the flare at the large plane. When he pulls the trigger, it's like setting off a firecracker.

A stream of smoke shoots into the air . . . but it's way too far to the left, behind the plane. The flare arcs and trails down. Not very bright or high.

And the plane continues its course. No sign. No dipping of wings. Nothing.

"Come back!" Land wails.

"They are way too far away," I say.

"How do you know?" he yells at me. "What makes you so smart all the time?"

Doc takes a deep breath. "How many shells do we have left?"

"Three."

Doc frowns but his voice stays even. "Go check on that ELT. And see if there's anything else that will burn. The firs are no good."

I head back with Land and crawl into the tail of the Cessna where the ELT is stashed. It's dark back there but I have matches in my pocket. I could light one and see the switch. My head swirls for a second. I take a breath. The air still smells of fuel.

No lighting matches, stupid, the plane will explode.

"If the Cessna had blown up before, that would have got that pilot's attention," I tell Land.

"Stupid plane. Never does what it's supposed to."

"Yeah," I agree. "You know what, it's too dark in here. We need a flashlight. I don't want to turn off the ELT signal if I guess wrong."

As we stumble out of the airplane, I stop to stare at that small pond of blue liquid under the wing. And I get an idea.

"That's it!" I tell Land. "Let's dip some of our branches in the avgas. They should go up like crazy."

We run back to the trees and grab several branches.

"How was the signal?" Doc Joe asks.

"I needed a light. I couldn't tell."

"Did you check the survival kit? There must be a flashlight in there."

"Give me a minute here," I tell him.

"Listen, I'm going to start the fire, first. The ELT can wait." I shred a carton and place it over a roll of toilet paper. On top of that I pile the fuel-soaked branches. Squatting, I light the toilet paper. The paper blazes bright, the carton flames more slowly. Suddenly there's a loud *poof.*

Chapter 7
Invisible

THE FLAMES FEEL so hot against my face, I forget all the rest. I stand and pile more branches on. Because of the intense heat, they catch too. Still on my feet, I close my eyes and feel myself swirling. I could just lie down and sleep in front of it.

"The ELT signal," Doc Joe nags. He's sitting next to Mom.

I'm so tired, I snap at him. "Just because you can't do a thing with those broken arms, doesn't mean I've grown an extra pair."

Land scrambles to the survival kit and digs through the stuff. He doesn't want to be in on this.

Doc Joe backs off. "I'm sorry, Sky." He glances

over at Mom and then back at me. I can almost sense what he wants to tell me, but I don't want to hear. He lowers his voice. "It's true. I can't do a thing for you." I hear his heavy sigh. "Worse, I can't do anything for your mom." He stares up at the swirling snow above us and blinks a few times.

Don't cry, don't cry, don't cry. You know you're in big trouble when an adult tears up. So as long as Doc Joe holds it together, I can too.

"While you were in the Cessna, another plane passed."

"And they didn't see us either," I say. *It's the ELT,* I tell myself. *It's not working, and I didn't check it.*

Doc shakes his head. "The Cessna is white. Against the snow, it's hard to spot. And we're hidden by trees." He drops his voice even lower as he glances at my brother and then back at me. "Your mom needs a hospital."

I nod. He doesn't have to tell me. She's in a pretty bad way. I wipe my eyes and sniff. It's important for Land that I not cry.

"Found the flashlight," my brother interrupts.

"Great," I say. "Let's go back to the plane. Grab that stupid orange garbage bag too." Angry works better for me, than sad. Right now, I'm angry at myself.

Land snaps the tent down and rushes to keep up with me.

I talk as I march. "See if you can tie it to the Cessna somehow. Maybe those search and rescue people will see us then."

Land struggles with the tent. I climb into the plane and crawl back into the tail. Flicking on the flashlight, I train it onto a yellow box. The switch plate is labeled *Arm/Off/On*. The toggle leans towards Arm. What does that even mean? We want it *On* don't we? I follow the instructions to reset, flicking it from *Arm* to *Off* then *On*. The yellow box stays silent. I keep flicking the switch, feeling stupid.

At the end, I leave it pushed toward *On*.

Land sticks his head in. "I opened the tent and

hung it around the wing. Only place it would stay."

"You did great. Doesn't matter what part of the plane the SAR team sees." I make my way to the front to join him. "Here, let's pull out these headrests. They may burn." I tell him. I yank out the one from Mom's seat. Land pulls out Doc Joe's.

I stare at his empty chair for a moment. It lies flat out like a bed. The co-pilot's seat, where I wanted to sit. The instrument panel is crunched in. It should have been me with the broken arm and hand that Doc has. But Mom wouldn't let me sit there. She's smart, that mom of mine. And I was so mad at her at the time.

Land and I return to the fire, and I hurl her headrest into the flames. The sparks fly up.

Doc Joe looks at me, his eyebrow raised in a question.

I shrug. "I switched the ELT on. I don't know if the thing is dead or not. I can't hear a thing."

"We won't hear it. Other pilots might."

Might.

"Why didn't Mom turn the signal on?" Land asks.

"Shouldn't matter," Doc says. "It's supposed to go off on its own when we crash."

"And Mom logged a flight plan with the airport," I add. "They'll know where we are."

Doc Joe screws up his mouth. "Sure she did. We just flew slightly off course when we hit that storm."

Great. Nobody really knows where we are.

Land scoops up a mittful of snow and leans forward to eat it.

"Don't!" I bash his hand, sending the snow flying.

"Ow. I'm thirsty!" he whines.

"You'll get too cold," I tell him.

"You said you would find more water."

"You're right. Why don't you dump all the bags? One of them's got to have a bottle of water in it. Meanwhile I'll make us some pine needle tea."

In the survival kit I find a pot and some water

purification tablets. Because we can melt the snow, we don't need those pills. But there are also four protein bars. I unwrap one and offer it to Doc.

"Don't think I can eat, but I'll have some of that tea you're making."

With the pot in hand, I scoop up some snow. Then I place the pot square into the fire, take a bite of the protein bar and sigh. It's dry with a hint of apple. Delicious today. Even though the pot is full of snow, it will all melt down to a cup or so. This will take forever.

Still what else do we have to do?

"What about using Diamond Lodge's pail?" Land suggests. He digs it from their carton and pitches it to me.

That kid must get his smarts from Mom.

When I finish packing it with snow, I set it in the flames too. "Come have a protein bar."

"Yuck," Land says. "That's okay. I have some chocolate peanut butter ones Auntie Fran gave me."

Auntie Fran is his after-school sitter on days

when I have band practice. "Chocolate peanut butter! You rat! Give me some!"

He hands me one and chows down on one himself. "Doc, you want one?"

"No, thanks."

The only meal we've had today was dry cereal, yet Doc Joe doesn't want to eat. Or maybe can't eat. I remember the mangled dash over the co-pilot seat. Doc Joe has to be injured pretty bad. At least as bad as Mom, and she lies there unconscious. What if we lose him too?

Chapter 8
Time's Running Out

"WHEN WILL THEY come for us?" Land asks. He's staring up at the dull gray sky. The wind blows the snow into a blur across it. "Shouldn't they be here by now?"

Doc can only shrug one shoulder. "Your mom put in the Mayday. The lodge knows we're late. It's just about the visibility. If the SAR team can't see, there's no point in them flying out for us."

"There's only a couple of hours of daylight left," I say looking up too. "We'll have to bunk down for the night."

Land reaches into his pocket and pulls out a tissue, unfolding it carefully. "If I put my tooth under my pillow out here, will the Tooth Fairy come?"

Are you kidding me? All this, and the kid is worried about the Tooth Fairy?

"I don't know, buddy," Doc answers. "Do you think she can see through the snow better than the search and rescue guys?"

"Why don't you worry about what you're going to use for a pillow? Keep looking through the luggage. Maybe you'll find us a nice warm sleeping bag or two. And just in case, I'm going to cut some more branches for a mattress."

I know what's in my bag—all my summer stuff. I was ready for L.A. and Disneyland, not this. But this is what we have. I cut more branches, then cover the ground with them. I pile all my shorts and t-shirts on top. They make okay sheets. At the end, it's a kind of bed. It has to be.

Land goes through Doc's bag, throwing out some sweaters. When he hits his underwear, he takes off his monkey hat and pulls a pair of briefs over his head. His eyes peek through the leg holes.

"Hey, Captain Underpants, give me those," Doc says weakly. Then he laughs. Not a good idea. Doc ends up coughing too long and turning gray. When he turns away from us, I see him spit out blood.

To distract Land, I pull some underwear over my head, too. He giggles. It's a nice sound, and it makes me feel guilty for being mad before. I decide I will find five dollars to slip under his pillow for that tooth of his. The Tooth Fairy has to find us, snow or not.

"Water's ready for the pine needles," Doc says.

The snow in the small pot has melted. Now it's heated into water that bubbles and pops. I pull off some needles from a branch and pitch them in.

"There's hot chocolate in one of the Lodge's boxes," Land says. He reaches into one box and brings out a few packets, luxury stuff, made with real dried cream.

"Is there a cup in there too?" I ask, peeling the briefs from my head. We have all this water and instant hot chocolate mix, but nothing to drink it in.

"I had a thermos of coffee in the cockpit," Doc says. "Your mom, too."

"It's probably cold by now," Land says.

"Yeah, but we could dump it and pour the hot water in," I tell him. "Wouldn't you rather have hot chocolate than pine needle tea?"

So we jog back to the plane and look under the seats. Mom's thermos is way in the back but Land crawls after it. Doc's is wedged under his seat. I poke it out with a knife and we head back.

Then I get creative. With a couple of pairs of socks, I'm able to hold up the hot pail. Then I pour the boiling water over the hot chocolate in the thermos.

Doc doesn't want the chocolate, so I pour the pine needle tea for him. When it cools a little, I hold it for him till he has a good long drink. It's too difficult for him to lift the cup himself. Land sips from the cup part of Mom's thermos, I sip from the container part. Over the rustle of the flames, I hear Mom's breath. It's hard and rattles.

Doc holds her hand. I see a tenderness in his eyes and watch his lips move as he whispers to her. In the quiet, I realize he's not saying "I trust you." He's saying "I love you."

"Are you going to be our new dad?" Land asks.

I gasp. Land's words sound matter-of-fact. Somehow he must already know about the divorce.

"Nobody is replacing your father," Doc answers. He's not denying it.

"How could you?" I sputter.

"Listen, both of you," Doc says weakly. "Your mom and I grew up together. Your dad was the southern stranger who stole her heart. She's not leaving him for me."

"Dad's leaving Mom because he hates the cold," Land explains to me. He shocks me again with how well he's taking this.

"Your mom and dad had a two-year plan," Doc says. "Your mom wanted to leave Hay River when she first came to the North."

"Why didn't they?" I ask.

"Your dad needed to get a little teaching experience first. Then your mom went for her pilot's license. She needed flying time. Two years became four. She had you guys . . ."

"And then she never wanted to leave," I finish for him.

Doc nods. "She loves her job. But your father has had enough. You either love the North or you don't."

"And he doesn't." I swallow back tears. "It's not fair."

"No, it's not. It's just life. Come sit by your mother." He points to her other side. "You should talk to her."

"She doesn't look like she's in any shape to be listening."

He raises his eyebrows at me as we listen to her breathing, slow and hard. "Well, she can't talk back, but I bet she can hear. Tell her anything you need her to know . . ." His voice trails off.

While you still have the chance. I don't make a big deal of the situation for Land's sake. I spread out a jacket beside her and sit. Then I take her other hand. "Mom, you know I didn't mean what I said back on the tarmac."

Land stares at me big-eyed through those underpants. If this all wasn't so sad, that look would make me laugh.

I continue talking. "I only said it because you won't let me stay with you. I don't want to move away with Dad." I look up at Land.

Land hurls himself on top of me and hugs me.

"It's going to be okay," I pat his back. "You and me, we'll always be together."

He leans over to bury his head on Mom's shoulder. "You have to get better. Please, Mom!"

He understands what Doc is saying, too. No Tooth Fairy or Santa Claus will turn this around for Mom. She can't possibly make it until morning, and SAR won't fly in the dark.

Still leaning on Mom, Land cries softly and I rub his back. As Doc and I sip at our tea and hot chocolate, we stare over the fire. The sun makes that orangey-gold line appear around us again. It's setting.

Chapter 9
Yellow Eyes

AFTER HE'S CRIED himself out, I tuck Land into bed. Well, kind of a bed. It's a pile of clothes on pine needles. For his pillow, I plump up my backpack. Last minute, Land sits up and hands me his tooth, still wrapped in that tissue. I put it under the backpack.

Then Land lies back down. "I can't sleep," he complains, even though his eyes look heavy. "Read me a story."

"I don't have anything to read to you."

"Yes, you do. Read me *Zombie Polar Bear*," he says.

"It's too scary for seven-year-olds."

"Please?"

He's beat and will fall asleep in a minute or two. So I shuffle some clothes to find the book, then crack it open. "Zombie Polar Bear," I begin. I read the author's name and all the other stuff in front to drag it out. But Land is still awake.

So I start. "The large white bear lay dead on the trailer. His fur was pink from the bullet wound at his neck. As Jane leaned over to begin skinning him, a low moan came from his throat. Was it some kind of sound the body made after it was dead? Jane could almost swear the bear's head moved.

"'The polar bear couldn't still be alive,' Jane thought. 'Nothing could survive that gunshot.'"

I read on and on till the end of the chapter. That's when the hunters find themselves surrounded by pairs of yellow eyes. "Whoa, how are they going to get out of that one, eh, Land?" I look over at my brother. He's snoring softly.

Now it's time for the Tooth Fairy to do her thing. But I can only find two dimes in my pockets.

"Doc?" I call softly, but he looks to be asleep too. *Mom must have some money*, I tell myself. Ever so gently, I slip my hands into her parka pockets. Nothing. She must have a wallet somewhere. I get up and paw through all the clothes scattered around.

Can't find it. I look through her bag. No wallet there.

Doc stirs. "What are you looking for?" he asks.

"I need some cash to give Land from the Tooth Fairy. Do you have five bucks?"

"Can you grab my wallet from my jacket?" he asks.

I reach in and pull out a billfold. "Empty," I say.

"Look in the slot with my credit card. My lucky toonie should be there." Doc starts coughing.

Sure enough. It's a large shiny coin with a polar bear—silver on the outside, sunny gold in the middle. Even if it's only two dollars, Land will be a happy kid.

"First money I earned as a doctor," Doc says.

"I delivered a baby way out of town. The family wanted to give me something. It was either the toonie or a load of dried moose strips." Doc rasps and then spits to the side. "I thought the family would need that moose over the winter. So I took the toonie instead."

There's blood on the snow next to Doc. *Guess the good luck didn't last,* I think.

"Go on! Put the coin under Land's head," Doc says. "Give me the tooth instead." He winks at me and smiles. "Maybe it will bring me better luck."

Anything has to be better than this, I think.

I smile back at Doc and make the swap. Then I stoke up the fire with the prongs of the last headrest. When the sparks stir back into life, I throw the whole headrest in. That should keep the flames going for a little while. I settle down on my own pine-branch bed. I'm next to Mom. Her rattling breath becomes a kind of music. After all, the rattle means she's still alive.

I close my eyes and start to dream. Images of

that polar bear on Doc's lucky coin blend with the zombie on the cover of my book.

In my sleep I see the polar bear approach our fire. The bear is moaning, lurching, head tilting to one side. Its eyes glow. The sockets around his eyes are dark and sunken. There's blood dripping from fangs that have no lips covering them anymore. Part of me knows this has to be a nightmare. But part of me is there, in the dream. I hear moaning and I shudder. It all seems so real, too real.

Suddenly, I'm awake. The moaning is real. Doc is doing it. And a real pair of yellow eyes are staring back at me from just beyond the glowing coals. I blink a few times to clear the sleep away. The yellow eyes spark brighter than the embers. My breath speeds up. How do you kill a zombie bear? We don't have a weapon. Wait a minute. I toss aside clothes till I find the survival kit. I pull out the signal gun, crack it open, load it, take aim . . .

And blast the thing!

There's a loud shot. But the signal shell doesn't go where I aimed. More to the right.

Something yelps and yips, and the eyes disappear.

Doc lifts his head. "What happened?"

Land is awake, too. "Did a plane fly by?"

"No. I woke up and saw . . . a wolf." I don't want to tell them about my zombie dream. "He watched our fire for a long time, so I thought he might attack."

"Did you get him?" Doc asks.

"I don't know." I fumble in the clothes for the flashlight. Then I flick it on and sweep the light across the snow. Nothing. Just a long wisp of dying smoke. "He's gone, anyway."

"You did the right thing," Doc says. "He won't be back any time soon." Doc shivers as he looks around. "Fire's almost out. Better add more wood."

I stumble to my feet, stoke the embers and add a couple of rolls of toilet paper—plenty of that left. When it flames up, I add more branches. The needles light up and the branches crackle. I glance over at Mom. Doc looks over at her, too.

The IV bag is down to its last bit. Mom is still breathing though, louder than ever.

"You need to switch the bag," Doc tells me. "We can't let it run dry."

"How do I do that?"

"Easy. Turn off the pump for a second."

Easy for him. Still, I reach up to the branch and shut the tube.

"Great. Take out the stopper on the new bag. And switch the tube over to it."

Not half as bad as sticking needles in people's arms. Doc's right. It is easy.

"Now turn the pump on again. Adjust the nozzle. She shouldn't need quite so much fluid. That way this bag will last till the morning."

"Then what?" I ask.

"First light, we have to get SAR to see us." Doc frowns at the flare gun. "Only two bullets left. Let's not waste them."

Chapter 10
Choking

IT'S HARD TO FALL asleep again. I keep thinking about those yellow eyes out there, still watching me. Maybe joined by more pairs of eyes. A pack of starving wolves smelling Doc and my mother's blood. They're circling, coming in for the kill.

Better to think about the real world. Or is it? What if a snowstorm delays SAR again? Just how badly is Doc doing? What if the searchers never find us? And the worst thought: what if Mom is gone when I wake up? I reach under the blankets to find the pulse point at her wrist. The faint bumping under my fingers drums back some hope and lulls me to sleep.

"You can't fool me!" Land's voice wakes both Doc and me. It's the next morning. Land is sitting staring at the toonie under his backpack pillow. "The Tooth Fairy didn't bring this. It's Doc Joe's lucky coin."

"Sure, she brought it. What are you talking about?" I sit up and rub my eyes. The air feels slightly warmer but it's still snowing. The sky is a hazy gray. No sunlight makes it through. Can a pilot see in this?

"Doc told me all about this toonie. He got it for helping a lady have her baby." Land picks it up and winds his arm. It's as though he's going to pitch the coin. "There is no Tooth Fairy!"

I grab him to stop the throw. "Land, the Tooth Fairy brought you that coin for good luck. Don't you dare throw it away."

"It can't be lucky. Doc's hurt really bad."

"Hey, I'm alive," Doc grumbles. "How many people can say that after a plane crash?"

Land doesn't look so sure now.

I keep my grip on his arm. "Give the coin to Mom," I tell him gently. "She can use it."

Land's eyes grow big, and then he smiles. So easy to cheer him up. Eagerly he tucks the toonie into Mom's pocket. But then his face changes again. His eyes squeeze together and his mouth opens. "Mom can't breathe. Doc, help!"

He's right. Mom's making this awful gurgling sound.

"She's choking!" Doc says. With his good hand, Doc pries open Mom's mouth. "Sky, check if there's anything there. You've got to pull it out."

I take a breath and lean close. "I can't see past her tongue. It looks swollen."

"She needs a tracheotomy," Doc says. "And I can't do one."

A tracheotomy. The word turns my stomach. A scene from some movie plays in my mind. A guy opens a ball point pen, takes out the insides, and stabs the tube into a choking victim's throat.

That was a tracheotomy, I'm sure. After seeing the movie, I ran to the toilet and puked.

"You have to do it. I can guide you," Doc tells me.

"I . . . I can't."

"She'll die if we don't try."

"I'll do it," Land chimes in.

My brave little brother. I usually peel his apples for him.

But Land is forcing me to be strong.

I swallow . . . hard. "That's okay. Tell me what to do, Doc."

"You'll faint in the middle," Land says. And he may be right.

"No, I won't," I tell him. I try to sound certain.

"We don't have time for arguing," Doc snaps. "Amy's not getting any air." Doc takes a breath himself and speaks more calmly. "Get the scalpel from my bag. And grab the trach kit. Use the rubbing alcohol."

We move quickly. I wipe down Mom's throat.

"Just below her Adam's apple. Use your fingers to find the spot."

Mom sputters and gasps for air. She's turning blue. I can't work fast enough. Her neck feels cold beneath my fingers.

"You need to make a small cut. Deep though. It has to go through all three layers: skin, fat and ligament."

Stay in control, I tell myself. I inhale deeply and let my breath out slowly. Still I feel lightheaded.

"Now, Sky!" Doc says.

I press the blade into her throat. Blood bubbles up around it.

"Harder!" Doc shouts.

Sobbing, I blink a few times to clear my eyes and push the blade deeper. Tears stream down my face.

"That's it! Put the tube in!"

I grab the kit and insert the tube.

Instantly, Mom heaves a huge loud breath.

"You saved her!" Doc says. "You saved her life."

"Yeah, Sky!" Land cheers.

Easy for them to say. I'm still working hard to keep from puking. Doc keeps coaching me. "All right. Last thing, pack some gauze around the tube. Then use the medical tape to hold it all in place."

My head swirls as I snip the tape and place the gauze. My fingers feel clumsy. I so want to vomit. But I manage to finish the job. Mom's breathing. I did it!

I stagger away, past the fire, over to where the yellow eyes had been. That nightmare is over. Now there's real life. I throw up, and throw up. Heaving until there's nothing left inside me.

But over all that, I hear a drone somewhere in the distance. It's coming closer.

I search the clouds. Nothing. If I can't spot the plane, what are the chances the crew can spot us?

"Do you hear it?" Land calls to me. He lifts up the red signal gun.

"Point it high!" Doc commands.

"Wait for me to do it!" I run towards him.

We see the plane through the white of the snow for maybe half a second. Land tracks it with the muzzle.

"No, no! It doesn't shoot straight. Aim to the left of where you want it to go. Let me do it!"

Too late. Land pulls the trigger shooting a trail of smoke and fire behind the clouds.

"Nowhere near it," I say. "Why didn't you wait for me?"

"You were too slow!"

"It would be a miracle if they saw it," Doc says.

Land frowns. "Well, they should be looking for it."

"It doesn't matter who's at fault," I tell him. "Mom needs a hospital, now!"

Both Doc and I are staring at Land, and the kid looks like he's going to cry. But there's no time for that. Mom begins to make that gurgling noise again.

"Quick!" Doc says. "There's blood in the tube. Grab the bulb that came in the trach kit."

"This thing?" I snap up a turkey-baster-like bulb.

"Yes. Squeeze it first to empty the air."

I press my thumb and forefinger together on either side of the bulb.

"Now insert it."

I stick the pointed end into the tube.

"And release the bulb to draw the blood up."

I let go slowly.

"Great! Take it out, then squeeze it to empty it."

I remove the bulb and squeeze. Blood squirts all over the snow.

Oh my God, my holy God! I want to throw up but Mom's still gurgling.

"Do it again!" Doc Joe shouts at me.

Chapter 11
Abandoned

"SHE'S BREATHING again," Doc says. "You did great!"

My worst nightmare. I cut my mother's neck open. Stabbed her with a tube. Then I bled her to keep her breathing. Yeah, I did great. For now. But we can't keep going like this. One step away from the fire and it's bitter cold. If Mom dies, I just can't handle it anymore. I can't be strong for Land. I will just lie down beside her and die too.

Mom is going to die without help. I'm going to die if I have to siphon blood from her again. At least I'm going to want to die. That's the worst of it.

Losing hope.

Wanting to die.

Even though the search and rescue people must have some idea where we are. Even though we shoot flares. They can't find us. Too snowy. When the snow stops, the temperature will drop again, and it's not that warm anyway.

"They're never going to find us," Land sobs. "Are they?" He's lost hope too.

"This is too much." Doc scrambles up on his feet. "I'm going for help."

"No!" I blink twice and shake my head. "That's crazy!" I tell him. "You know the emergency drill. You always stay with the plane." *He can't leave us. He can't leave me!*

Doc looks at Mom and shakes his head. "This is a different emergency."

I get to my feet, too. "You can't go! You'll just get lost." I'm whining like a little kid now.

"Give me a break, Sky. I have some tracking skills. I can find my way over the land. If I'm right, we're not that far from Diamond Lodge."

"You're going to leave us all alone?" Land asks.

His voice is a whimper.

"I don't have a choice," Doc says. "Nobody can see us through that snow." Doc doubles over and coughs. Blood spatters onto the snow.

"This is stupid. You're not going to make it."

"Then I'll die trying," he says, like a line from an old movie. He looks away. "Sky, I love your mother. Always have, always will."

I knew, I guess, but there it is. Doc said it. I want to give him a hug but feel I can't move.

Doc kisses my forehead, nods at Land, and walks off.

Watching him, I feel a growing terror. It's all on me now. And I can't even breathe.

Land chases after him. "Don't go!" He dives for Doc's waist, and Doc hugs back as best he can.

"Look after yourself," Doc says and pulls away. "I'll find help. It won't be long."

"Land, come back here and stay with Mom and me," I say.

My brother cries little-boy sobs, and I throw my

arms around him, hugging him tight, tight. "Doc knows what he's doing," I lie. "He's going to be all right." How long can I keep faking for Land?

Over Land's head, I watch Doc walk off into the white snow and sky. He hasn't got a hope – I know that – but still he's trying. Somebody has to.

When he's gone, I rub my mitted hands together and try on a cheery voice. "I don't know about you, Land, but I'm on empty. What's to eat besides protein bars? Any bacon and eggs?"

The mere thought makes me want to throw up. But food is a great way to get Land's attention. He dashes back to our shelter near the rock and trees. He looks around in the black duffle kit, and comes up with a foil pouch that has a picture on the front. "Dried stuff in a bag." Land shakes it.

I grab it. "Macaroni and cheese for breakfast. Yum. We'll need a better fire to boil the water. Let's collect some more branches and dip them in avgas." Mom's IV bag is empty now but she keeps breathing through that trach tube. How long can she possibly have? *Help her, help her.* I don't know if I should take off the IV bag or leave it on, and Doc Joe isn't here to ask. *Please let him be okay*, I pray to no one in particular. *Please let Mom live.*

We've used all the lower branches of the trees nearby. Now we saw off a whole tree. Too green and fresh to burn? Not once we've rolled it in the avgas. Land helps me carry the tree over to the puddle near the Cessna. I dip it and we carry it back to the fire.

I unravel another roll of toilet paper onto the coals. "What are the tourists going to use to wipe their butts?" Land asks. I place some branches on top and pile more toilet paper on those.

"Maybe pine needles?" I laugh, *heh, heh, heh*, I can't stop. It's not that funny, but I'm losing it. At last I swallow a sob. "Stand back, I'm going to light this." I set the match to the toilet paper, then join Land.

As the flame licks at the avgas branches there's a mini *poof!*

"Too bad we weren't making breakfast when that last plane flew over," Land says.

I don't want to laugh again. I'll just end up crying. Instead I shake my head and look up. "If the sky cleared we wouldn't need an explosion." Still he gives me an idea. "We could soak some branches now." I think out loud. "When the next plane passes we can set them off to get their attention. But let me get the water started first for the macaroni."

I pack the pail with snow and place it in the fire to melt. Which makes me stop and think, Doc didn't even take any water with him. It would be too hard for him to open his thermos anyway what with his broken fingers and arm. Still how long can a person last without water? He can eat snow, I tell myself. He'll be fine.

No matches or food either, another voice inside me says. Doc is either that sure he'll find the Diamond lodge, or . . .

Land helps me saw down another fir tree. This one we roll in the avgas and set in the open. "Okay I'm going to give you the matches. If we hear a plane, you set it on fire and leap back." Who lets a seven-year-old set off an explosion? Someone desperate. Someone crazy. "Let me be in charge of the flare gun."

There's only one bullet left. I have to save it for the right moment. I load it into the small red gun. Even if a bear attacks, I'm not going to use it.

"Why don't you dust off the snow from that stupid tent on the wing," I tell Land. "I'll make us the macaroni."

Keeping busy is key so that we don't panic. I look at Mom. She's quiet but still breathing. Nothing more I can do for her.

Carefully, I tear open the pouch of macaroni. The package says to pour in two cups of boiling water, stir, then close the seal and wait. Simple. When the water in the pail bubbles, I scoop two thermos lids of it into the bag. Then I use my knife to stir.

So we wait. I can see our Cessna. The orange tent on the wing is showing now. And we have a gas-dipped tree ready to light up. All we need is a rescue plane.

The macaroni steeps. Land and I wait.

"Is it done yet?"

"No. Why don't you look for something else to eat?"

He digs around in the emergency bag. All he finds are a couple of plastic spoons. "Now is it done?"

"No."

"Will they come for us soon?" Land asks.

"Yes, any minute." Wishful thinking. I check the sky and wonder if the snow is letting up.

"Now is it ready?"

"Oh, fine." I'm just fed up, I don't even want to eat.

Dad makes the best macaroni and cheese. Sometimes he adds a little smoked char or moose meat. I'm sure this dried stuff can't be half as good. Still, my brother's hungry. I scoop some mac and cheese into Land's cup. I use Doc's lid for my own dish.

Land digs in. Crunch, crunch. He sounds like a Husky chewing kibble.

"A little under-done?" I ask.

"No. It's good."

I try some. It's tough and grainy. The macaroni is a sloppy salty orange mess of semi-cooked noodles. But I know that Land has to be starving. I keep eating, too. Keeps me from screaming.

We're almost done when my ears prick up. I hear a low rumble. "Land!" I shout.

"I'm going." He runs for the tree and pulls out a match.

"Be careful."

Land strikes the match a few times before it lights. Then he flings it onto the tree. *Poof!*

I pull out the bright red gun. I hold it in both hands, and pivot slowly watching for that plane. *Can't shoot too early*, I tell myself. This time it has to work.

And then I spot something else.

That puddle of avgas near the wing. Striking a match to a gas-soaked fir tree made a nice little *poof*. But what if I could get a bigger explosion? We

had a full tank leaving Hay River, and we weren't in the air long. If the flare hits the fuel, chances are the whole tank will blow.

The drone of the plane becomes louder now. The clouds part almost magically. I spot the plane in the sky. I could shoot up, like we planned, or . . .

I look over to that puddle of avgas, take aim and fire.

There's a one-second delay. Then a colossal explosion that shakes the snow beneath us.

Land falls backwards into the snow. Then he gives me a big thumbs up.

But the plane continues on. It's leaving us!

"Sky . . ." Land whines, looking at the plane.

We're both looking for a sign. A dip in one wing. Something.

We need something. The fuel is all gone. Doc Joe has disappeared. Mom's choking on her own blood. One more night and we'll freeze to death.

Chapter 12
Luck Runs Out

BUT THE PLANE did see us. It turns around, mid-air, then comes zooming over our camp.

"They see us!" I scream. "They see us!"

Of course that plane can't land here. The land is too rough, too uneven. They'd end up in the same shape as Mom's Cessna. But they know exactly where we are now. Rescue can't be far off.

I kneel down beside Mom. "It won't be long. You're going to get the help you need." They're coming for us."

She looks awful with her swollen bruised face and crusted wound. Even if she can hear me, she can't answer with that trach tube in her throat. And where is Doc Joe? Did the SAR team spot him too?

I run in the direction that Doc was heading. "Come back, Doc! They've spotted us. They're coming!"

Come back, come back, come back. Empty words in the wind. Nobody answers me. *Please be safe, Doc. Please be alive.*

Time passes slowly when you're waiting for someone to save your mom. I go back to our shelter and gather our stuff together. We won't be able to carry much of it back, but still. I grab *Zombie Polar Bear* and tuck it in my jacket. I'm glad I didn't have to burn my book. Land finishes up the last of the kibble macaroni.

Some time later, we hear the *whoot, whoot* of helicopter blades.

The snow finally stops, and we see a patch of blue in the sky. And through that blue, our rescue!

The helicopter hovers closer. We can see the pilot and the crew. One of them waves. The uneven rumble of the engine becomes louder. The chopper doesn't need a big runway like a plane. It can use a small flat patch safely away from the two fires we made.

The helicopter lands, bobbing back and forth. The blades make a wind that blows away some of the clothing we've been using as blankets. Some of the crew jump out, ducking their heads as they run. Each carries a large bag.

I rush them over to Mom. One unpacks his kit and hooks up a new IV pouch. He holds it up as the other checks her vital signs. They're looking at the tube in her throat. "Who did all this?"

"Me," I say. I don't know if I should feel guilty or proud. "She was choking. Doc Joe told me what to do."

"Doc Joe?" asks one of them.

"Did you see him? He walked off to get help about half an hour ago."

"No. But we'll watch for him on our way out." They unroll a stretcher and carefully lift Mom on. Together they hoist her up and head to the chopper.

"Keep your head down," the crew warns us as we scramble behind them. Land and I climb into the helicopter after Mom.

"We're taking your mother right to the hospital," one shouts to us.

I nod. The noise of the engine and blades makes it impossible to explain anything.

Still, I try. "But we need to look for Doc Joe!" I yell. "He's hurt pretty bad."

Whether the pilot hears or not, we lift off. I keep my eyes down, searching, searching. Trees, rocks, brown stumps . . . And then I see him.

"Over there!" I shout. "Over there!"

Doc Joe didn't make it all that far.

I see him on the ground . . . face down, curled up. He could just be a bundle of clothing. Except I recognize his parka. And there's a large reddish brown stain around his head.

I start shaking. My teeth chatter.

The helicopter lowers and lands again.

One crew member touches my arm. "Stay here."

I want to jump out after him, but I know I can't
help. I might even get in the way. So I watch as
they kneel down beside Doc Joe. One reaches his
hand around Doc's neck, checking for a pulse.

There's a quick head shake between them.

No!

Chapter 13
Learning to Smile Again

DAD LOOKS LIKE WE'VE come back from the dead. He's so happy to see us, he's ready to buy us a herd of horses.

"C'mon, Sky, it's over. Can you smile just a little?" he says.

But it's hard, you know.

You live your whole life and nothing bad happens. It's easy to be a kid then, smile and pretend to believe in Santa Claus and the Tooth Fairy. Then your parents split up and you think it's the worst thing. Your smile comes a little slower. But when someone close to you dies, you know that divorce is nothing.

Sometimes I feel like I'm a hundred years old now. And my little brother seems like he's turned fifty. I haven't heard him giggle in ages. He still checks that Mom has Doc Joe's toonie. So maybe he still believes in good luck charms. I know he still believes in the Tooth Fairy.

My face feels stiff. I can't smile, at least not yet. But the headaches are going away. The new doctor says I shouldn't have any long-term damage. And she's impressed with my surgery skills. Says I should become a doctor or a nurse.

No way.

We visit Mom in the hospital, and she's getting better every day. Who cares about the big scar on her face? She's alive. Maybe her voice is a little raspy, but she's still here. A miracle, of some sort. Dad says she may have a career as a jazz singer.

I don't know if Mom will want to fly again as a bush pilot. So instead of living in Hay River without us, she'll probably end up living down south. Closer. And maybe that's okay. I don't know how I feel about the North any more. Beautiful as it is, it was Doc Joe's killer.

Of course, we're all going to fly back to Hay River for Doc's service. But it won't be the same. This time a large Air Canada plane will take us to Yellowknife. Then a smaller transfer plane will get us to Hay River. We won't even see the cockpit.

I'm sure a lot of people will turn up for the service, and that will be nice. Josée and her boyfriend will be there. And a lot of kids from the school. Doc Joe was loved by all of his patients.

Maybe by me, too. I sure miss him. I wish I could have stopped him from heading off that day. Sometimes I wonder if that would have helped. Right from the plane crash, I thought he was injured worse than he was letting on. It was just like him to act strong for our sakes. And for Mom's. Doc had to stay strong to help us. No way Mom would have lived without him guiding me through that tracheotomy. When he left to get help, I had a feeling it would be the last time we saw him. I think we both knew he was walking off to die.

I remember his smile just before he left. And his words: *I love your mother. Always have, always will.*

Someday that won't make me cry.

I also remember him taking my seat in the front. The pilot and co-pilot always take it the worst in a crash. It could have been me, all crushed inside. Maybe it should have been me.

Sometimes I still hear his voice. I can hear him say, "You can survive this, too."

I believe I will. And I will smile again, one day soon.

Acknowledgements

The author wants to offer special thanks to the specialists who helped with the research and the fact-checking for this novel.

Dr. Frank Fornasier, Joseph Brant Hospital
Susan Smiley, retired ER nurse
Anita Daher, writer and former flight specialist
Capt. Keith Murdock, Civil Aviation Safety Inspector
Dr. Orest Skrypuch, pilot

About the Author

SYLVIA McNICOLL is the author of the "Bringing Up Beauty" series about guide dogs, as well as the novel *Dog on Trial* for HIP Books. She has also written almost thirty other novels for young people. Her most recent young adult novel is called *Crush. Candy. Corpse.*

Sylvia has taught creative writing at Sheridan College, edited *Today's Parent Toronto* and acted as an electronic writer-in-residence. She visits libraries and schools giving writing workshops and presentations to inspire reading and writing. Visit her website at www.sylviamcnicoll.com.